Misha Supe. _

Foreword

These stories were made up as bedtime tales for my new grand-daughter, Evelyn.

As with my other books, the stories here are based partly on family experiences and partly on things I would like to be possible.

Misha was the name of our family cat.

Gerard was the name of our neighbour's pet cat.

Both sadly missed.

Once again, my thanks go to Anne Hulse for bringing the characters to life in such a clever and thoughtful way.

I hope you enjoy their adventures.

GJ Abercrombie

Edinburgh

2019

For Evelyn

Chapter 1

Meet Misha

Misha Cat lives in Edinburgh with her 'owners', Mr and Mrs Macdonald.

As you may know, you never really 'own' a cat. A cat will do exactly what it likes and will come and go as it pleases. As long as you feed it regularly and give it somewhere to sleep, it will be happy to let you think of yourself as its 'owner'.

Misha Cat does all of these 'normal cat' things ... but there's more!

She has a secret which only one other creature in the world knows about.

This other creature happens to be a cat too. He is her friend, Gerard, and he lives and works in the shop downstairs from Misha's flat. Misha lets the Macdonalds believe it is their flat but she knows it is really hers.

Misha's secret is that she is really a superhero. She is MISHA SUPERCAT!

All day long, Misha pretends to be asleep on a cushion on the wide window-sill of the bay window in the front room of the flat.

She purrs gently.

Every now and then she stretches and turns round to face the other way.

She looks just like any other lazy pet cat having a snooze …

… but all the time she is wide awake and ready to spring into action when needed.

She keeps one eye on the big mirror which hangs above the fireplace …

Watching and waiting and listening!

(What is she waiting for? You'll find out in a minute!)

Misha likes helping people (and other animals).

Whenever anyone is in trouble they can count on Misha Supercat to come to the rescue. All they have to do is to ask for her help.

(How do they do that, you ask?)

In order to request help from Misha Supercat, all you have to do is to find the nearest pedestrian crossing and press the button three times, very quickly.

The traffic lights for the cars will all come on at the same time, RED, AMBER and GREEN.

For people crossing the road, both the RED man and GREEN man signs will come on too.

This lets everyone know that Misha Supercat has got the message and help is on its way.

Now, here is why Misha watches the big mirror and listens so carefully …

As soon as the traffic light button is pressed three times and the lights all come on, the mirror makes a loud 'PING'. It sounds just like a microwave oven.

At the same time, a map appears on the glass of the mirror!

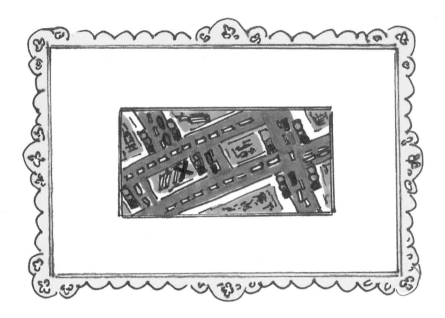

The map on the mirror has a big X on it to show Misha Cat the exact place where Misha Supercat is needed.

(Can you see the X on this map?)

Every time the mirror makes its 'PING', Mr Macdonald thinks that it's the microwave oven. He goes into the kitchen and opens the door of the microwave to see if some food is ready.

He is always very confused when he sees it is empty!

When the mirror pings and the map appears, it is time for Misha to be transformed in Misha Supercat!

(We'll find out how Misha Cat becomes Misha Supercat next time.)

Chapter 2

Supercats to the Rescue

Most of the time, Misha looks like a normal pet cat.

Her fur is mostly white with black and grey patches and she wears a pink collar around her neck.

Now, as you know, every superhero needs a disguise.

When Misha Cat turns into Misha Supercat, the black patches on her fur spread over her whole body to turn her into an all-black cat. This is her secret disguise!

After she has transformed, Misha Supercat runs to the back window of the flat and presses a secret button which is hidden behind the curtains.

It does not really matter if Mr and Mrs Macdonald see her running past because she does not look like their cat anymore. They just think it is a cat-friend who has come to visit Misha.

When Misha presses the hidden button, the window slides open and the drain-pipe attached to the wall outside starts to swing out over the garden below.

At the same time a bouncy, rubber cover, like a trampoline, slips out over the fish-pond. Misha slides down the drain-pipe, lands on the fish-pond cover and bounces up into the air.

As she does this, her pink collar unravels to form a cape which helps her to fly! The cape has the letters 'MS' for Misha Supercat on it. She then soars over the garden fence and zooms off to wherever she is needed.

Gerard from the shop downstairs is Misha's side-kick. He is a red cat. Some people call it Ginger.

Gerard's shop downstairs sells all sorts of tools: saws and hammers, chisels and screwdrivers as well as paint, nails and screws.

On the wall of the tool-shop, there is a big picture of Gerard's Auntie Kate. She is a famous dancer and the picture shows her in her ballet outfit. It looks just like an ordinary portrait of her in a pretty dress and ballet-shoes but it is secretly connected to the mirror upstairs.

Whenever the mirror pings and the map appears, his Auntie Kate's ballet-shoes in the picture start to flash silver. This tells Gerard that the Supercats are needed somewhere.

Gerard locks the front door of the shop and turns the sign on it to read 'CLOSED'.

He uses a scooter to follow Misha Supercat as she flies off to rescue people. His scooter is kept in a little shed in the garden by the back door of the shop.

His Supercat disguise is kept there too, on a shelf above the scooter.

Gerard's Supercat disguise is a gold-coloured cape and matching mask.

Gerard also keeps a special rucksack packed with tools ready for emergencies. He collects the tool-bag on his way out and puts on his gold mask and cape in the little shed outside.

Gerard Cat is then ready to join Misha Supercat in the lane at the back of the garden!

Gerard is not a REAL superhero, like Misha.

He would love to be a superhero one day, but, for now, he is just an ordinary cat.

His cape cannot make him fly so he always just opens the back gate to get out of the garden. It's a bit tricky getting the gate open when you have a scooter and a rucksack full of tools to balance at the same time.

One day, in his excitement to follow Misha, Gerard closed the gate too soon and caught his cape in the lock. When he set off on his scooter, he was suddenly jerked back by his neck.

He was nearly strangled!

"AYAH", he shouted and fell backwards onto the path. His scooter and rucksack landed on top of him.

He was embarrassed, but no-one could tell because his face is already red!

Gerard picked himself up and sorted his cape. He put his rucksack back onto the handlebars of his scooter and quickly looked around to see if anyone had seen him fall.

No-one had seen him; that was lucky!

Gerard was then ready to set off on the important mission.

Now, one of Misha's superhero skills is that she can always speak the language of the person or animal that needs to be rescued.

As she takes off into the air, Misha Supercat usually calls out in excitement.

It's normally something like:

"Misha Supercat to the rescue!"

Gerard can't speak human language so when he tries to shout:

"Gerard to the rescue!"

… it sounds like:

"MYEH-MYEH … MYEH … MYEH … MYEH-MYEH!".

He still sounds like a cat!

Gerard can understand other languages when he hears them spoken but he himself can only speak 'cat'. This annoys him a little but it was very useful one day; as we shall hear!

Chapter 3

Roof Rescue

One day, Misha Supercat and Gerard were called to a very strange rescue.

A man was stuck up on a roof and could not get down. He had climbed up a ladder to fix his chimney and while he was up there, the wind had blown his ladder over. It was lying on the pavement outside his house.

He managed to shout down to a small girl called Cora who was passing and asked her to call for help. Cora was very clever and knew how to contact Misha Supercat.

She ran to the nearest pedestrian crossing and pressed the button three times, very quickly. The lights all came on to show that the signal had been sent and so she waited there for Misha Supercat and Gerard to arrive.

Back in Misha's flat, the mirror pinged and a map appeared behind the glass. Mr Macdonald heard the 'PING' and thought:

"That will be my lunch ready."

But, when he opened the door of the microwave oven, there was nothing in it! *(Silly Mr Macdonald)*

The map showed the crossing in Corstorphine.

Misha dashed to the back window, her fur turning black as she ran. Her cape was fully unwrapped by the time she landed on the trampoline over the pond.

"Destination Corstorphine", shouted Misha as she took off.

"MYEH-MYEH-MYEH-MYEH … MYEH-MYEH-MYEH", echoed Gerard as he got on his scooter and tried to keep up with Misha.

Cora met them at the crossing and told them about the ladder. The two Supercats told her not to worry: they were on the job!

They picked up the ladder between them and held it tight with their claws (or clooks as they called them).

Unfortunately, Gerard is a bit clumsy. He is constantly dropping things or tripping over things.

As they were carrying the ladder towards the wall of the house, he tripped over and let go of his end.

His tools spilled out of his rucksack, all over the pavement and the ladder landed on Gerard's left foot.

"AYAH!" he shouted as he hopped about on his other foot.

Sadly, he hopped onto a screwdriver which had come out of the tool-bag and hurt his right foot.

"AYAH, AYAH!" he cried and sat down on the ground rubbing BOTH of his feet.

It took all of Misha's super-strength to try to hold the ladder up by herself, but she managed to place it back against the wall.

"OK, you can come down now. The ladder is quite safe", she announced.

The man climbed down and seemed very embarrassed about needing to be helped.

"There's no shame in asking for help", said Misha.

"Ah, but you see, I'm a fireman", said the man, "It's usually firemen who rescue cats who are stuck, not the other way round".

"MYEH, MYEH", said Gerard and he winked at Misha, who smiled back.

"What did he say?" asked the fireman.

(Remember, Gerard could only speak cat-language so the fireman did not understand him.)

Misha Supercat had to tell him what Gerard had said.

"Gerard says that you've not to worry.

We won't tell anyone that we had to rescue a fireman", explained Misha.

The fireman blushed a little, but he smiled and thanked Misha Supercat.

The rescued fireman started to pack away his ladder.

He gave Gerard a funny look as the clumsy cat started to pick up all of his tools and put them back into his rucksack.

"Another successful mission for the Supercats. Helping people in need, that our business", said Gerard.

"Yes, but some cats were more helpful that others", replied Misha.

Chapter 4

How Misha Met Gerard

This is the story of how Misha and Gerard first got together to form the Supercats.

For a long time, the shop downstairs from Misha's flat was empty. It had previously been a fruit and vegetable shop but people started buying all these things from supermarkets so the shop closed, which was a shame.

The fact that the shop was empty did mean that Misha Cat could change into Misha Supercat on her way down the stairs without being seen by anyone. She would then sneak out of the front door; hoping no-one would spot her. She did not want anyone to know where she lived. Misha would then run along the pavement until she was going fast enough to take off into the air, helped by her pink cape.

Then one day, Gerard bought the shop and filled it with tools and paint and lots of other handy things which supermarkets don't sell. He was hidden behind a pile of boxes when Misha was called out on a mission.

(Can you see Gerard?)

He was busy unpacking all his stuff and had just hung up the picture of his Auntie Kate on the wall when Misha came down the stairs.

She was opening out her cape just before going out of the door when Gerard saw her.

"My goodness", he exclaimed, "It's Misha Supercat! Do you live upstairs?"

"Well, yes. But, please don't tell anyone" she pleaded.

"OK", said Gerard, "but, can I be your assistant?"

"Oh, I suppose so", she replied although she suspected that he might be more of a pest than a help.

"I can't fly, like you can; but I have lots of handy tools which could help you in your rescues", he added.

Misha had never had an assistant before but she did agree that Gerard's tools might be handy to have.

So, they agreed that Gerard could help Misha.

He found an old gold-coloured curtain in one of his boxes and made a cape and a mask from it. He was very pleased with his new Supercat disguise but he knew that the cape was not a real superhero one.

Since his cape did not have any letters on it, Gerard knew he could not fly with it.

Misha explained about how the mirror upstairs would ping to alert her when someone needed help.

"You will need some kind of signal down here too", she said.

Gerard used his tools to connect the picture of his Auntie Kate to the map-mirror upstairs so that the ballet-shoes flashed when the mirror pinged.

Misha told Gerard that she would prefer to go out on missions through the back garden but the stairs from her flat only led to the front door.

"No problem", said Gerard, "I'll fix up an escape route for you".

Gerard loves inventing new things and building them himself; that is why he owns a tool-shop.

He used his tools to make the window open automatically and the drain-pipe swing out from the wall when the secret button behind the curtain is pressed.

He also made the trampoline cover for the pond in the garden.

"If you bounce up into the air on the trampoline, you'll not need to run along the pavement anymore", Gerard told Misha.

It took a few tries before everything worked properly. The first time Misha pushed the button, the drain-pipe swung out too far and she landed in a jaggy holly bush over by the gate. Gerard adjusted the mechanism and it then swung out over the pond.

But, there was a problem here too.

The cover did not slide out completely and Misha landed in the water!

She got soaking wet and had to dry herself with her cape while Gerard made 'minor adjustments' to the pond-cover mechanism.

Even when the equipment all worked, it still took Misha a few attempts to get into the air successfully.

The first time she tried it, she flew off to the side and landed in the holly bush AGAIN!

The second time, she bounced backwards and flew back in through the upstairs window of the flat.

Mr Macdonald was too busy looking in the microwave oven and scratching his head in confusion to notice a cat flying in through the window.

But on the third go, she managed to control the bounce and flew off over the houses with her cape flapping out behind her.

"This is much better than sneaking down the stairs and running along the pavement. Thanks Gerard!" she cried.

Gerard jumped on his scooter and followed her on the ground.

He thought to himself that he'd need to invent a way of making his scooter go faster so he could keep up with Misha Supercat.

(How do you think he might do that?)

Chapter 5

False Alarm

When Misha and Gerard first formed the Supercats, not many people knew about them or how to contact them in emergencies.

"We need to advertise ourselves", said Gerard.

"Let's design a poster and we can put it in all the shop windows in Edinburgh", said Misha.

So, they took photos of Misha (in her Misha Supercat disguise) and Gerard (in his cape and mask). They put the photos on a poster along with instructions about pressing the button at the crossing three times.

Gerard tried to hide the fact that his cape did not have any letters on it. He did not want people to know that he was not a <u>real</u> superhero.

Soon, the two friends were getting lots of calls for help; they were very busy.

One day, the mirror pinged and a map of Stockbridge appeared.

Mr Macdonald went and put on some oven-gloves before he opened the door of the microwave. He thought there would be something very hot inside and was surprised to find it empty (again).

Misha and Gerard rushed to the back garden.

"Destination Stockbridge", shouted Misha as she took off.

"MYEH-MYEH-MYEH-MYEH … MYEH-MYEH"

… shouted Gerard as he leapt on his scooter.

When they got to the scene of the emergency, they found a little girl called Esther with a new kitten.

"What's the problem?" asked Misha Supercat.

"Oh, there's no problem. I just wanted to ask you what food is best to feed my new pet", said Esther.

"That's not really an emergency, is it?" said Misha "Look at the traffic lights all lit up like a Christmas tree just so you can ask me about food!"

"But, I thought you could help me", said Esther, starting to cry.

Misha felt sorry for Esther (and the hungry kitten) so she suggested some nice fish cooked in warm milk for the kitten's dinner.

"MMMMMM", said Gerard, rubbing his tummy hungrily. That was one of his favourite meals.

On their way back home, Misha and Gerard had a chat about the problem of people wanting help and advice rather than needing to be rescued.

Then Misha had a good idea.

She remembered that you can phone '999' if you need the police in an emergency or you can phone '101' if it's not urgent.

"We should have a system like that too", she told Gerard.

So, they decided that if people pressed the crossing button TWICE instead of THREE times, the Supercats would be alerted but not for an emergency.

In this case, the RED and GREEN traffic lights for the cars would flash on and off one after the other.

The RED man and GREEN man signs for pedestrians would do the same. This would let everyone know that Misha Supercat had got the message and that help and advice were on their way.

They added these instructions to the posters in the shops so everyone would know the new rules.

Back in the flat, when a non-urgent request came in, the mirror would make a sneezing noise instead of a 'PING'. Also, in the tool-shop, Gerard's Auntie Kate's right shoe would flash in the photograph but the left shoe would not. This way both Supercats would know if the call was an emergency or not.

Mr Macdonald did not have to check the microwave oven when one of these calls came in but he kept on saying "Bless you, my dear" when he heard the mirror sneezing.

He did not know that it was the mirror making the noise.

He just thought that his wife had a bad cold!

Chapter 6

Scooter Booster

Gerard was having difficulty keeping up with Misha on his scooter.

She would zoom off at speed up in the air and he had to struggle along on the ground. He really wished he could fly like Misha.

"If only I could find a way to make my scooter go faster", he thought.

One evening, he was watching television in the room at the back of his shop where he lives. It was a programme about rockets. He noticed that their jet boosters made them go really fast.

"What could I use to make a jet booster for my scooter?" he wondered.

Then he had a 'good idea'.

He noticed that all the rocket boosters had hot air blowing out at the back. He remembered seeing something like that up in Misha's flat so he went upstairs to ask his friend about it.

Once Gerard had described the thing he had seen, Misha knew what it was. *(Can you guess what it was?)*

"That's Mrs Macdonald's hairdryer", she said.

"Do you think I could borrow it?" asked Gerard.

"I'm sure that will be fine", said Misha, "What do you want it for?"

"Oh, just a new experiment", he said, mysteriously.

He wanted to surprise Misha with his new speedy scooter so he decided to keep it secret for now.

Gerard took the hairdryer down to his tool-shop and started work straight away. He used two big brackets and four screws to attach the hairdryer to the back of the scooter. The hot air tube was facing backwards and the switches were on the top so he could reach them with his foot.

He decided to give it a try in the shop. He pushed himself along with his foot as usual to start the scooter moving. Once he was going, he pressed the button marked "1" with his toe. The hairdryer started making a whirring noise and some hot air came out of the back.

Gerard's scooter went a bit faster.

Then he pressed the button marked "2" and the whirring noise got louder. More hot air came out of the back and he sped up even more.

"Wee-Hee", he cried as he zoomed around his workshop.

"I'm going to try number 3", he thought and pressed the last button.

He suddenly shot forward and crashed into a big pile of cardboard boxes. These boxes were left over from when he had moved into the shop. They were all empty so he did not hurt himself.

He switched off the hairdryer-booster and tidied away all the boxes.

"Right, now I'm going to show Misha", he thought.

He shouted up the stairs:

"Hey, Misha! Look out of the back window and you'll see something exciting in the garden".

Misha went through to the back room and looked out of the window.

A few seconds later she saw Gerard come zooming out of the back door of his shop into the garden.

He was going at an incredible speed.

Suddenly, there was an enormous

TWANG

... and the scooter came to a sudden stop.

Gerard went flying over the handle-bars and landed in the jaggy holly bush by the back gate (the one Misha used to land in before she perfected her take-off technique).

Misha was worried for her friend and hurried down into the garden to check that Gerard was OK.

"Are you hurt, Gerard? What happened?"

"I don't know. I made a booster for my scooter so I could keep up with your flying. It worked fine in the shop", he moaned as he picked holly leaves out of his fur.

The two friends looked back towards the shop and saw a long wire running from the door to the scooter.

"Oh dear", said Gerard, "I forgot that the hairdryer had to be plugged into the wall for it to work. It was fine inside the shop but the cable is not long enough to reach across the garden."

"Well, if it needs to be plugged in, you won't be able to use it on missions. Will you?" Misha pointed out.

"I suppose not. I'll just have to think of another way to scoot faster", he sighed, rubbing his sore head.

(Poor old Gerard!)

Chapter 7

Chip Wars

One bright sunny day, Misha Cat was pretending to have a snooze, as usual.

Gerard was downstairs in his tool shop working on new inventions. He was still trying to work out a way to make his scooter go faster. He did a lot of experiments while the Supercats were not out on missions.

Suddenly there was a loud 'PING' from the mirror upstairs and Gerard's Auntie Kate's shoes <u>both</u> flashed silver.

(Do you remember what that means?)

There was an emergency!

Gerard quickly locked up the shop and headed for the back door.

He knew that Misha Supercat would be coming down the drain-pipe soon and he wanted to get to the path before she did.

He did not stop to put on his disguise but just grabbed it from the shelf in the shed.

He was struggling across the garden trying to put on his mask and cape while riding his scooter. Gerard's cape got stuck in the back wheel of the scooter just as he was passing the fish pond and he fell over.

He was about to land in the pond!

Luckily, the bouncy cover had already slid over the pond or else he would have fallen into the water.

But, not so luckily, Misha was sliding down the drain-pipe heading for the trampoline.

She landed right on top of Gerard!

"What are you doing, Gerard?" Misha exclaimed.

"I wanted to beat you to the back path so I could get a head start", he explained. "My scooter is so slow that I always have to follow you".

"But you don't even know where we're heading. You haven't seen the map on the mirror. How can you possibly lead the way?" Misha pointed out.

"Oops, silly me, I didn't think of that", said Gerard.

Misha had to climb back up the drain-pipe and slide down again to get a good bounce to take her over the fence and up into the air.

Gerard fixed his mask and cape which had come off when he fell over and waited for Misha at the back gate.

"Destination Portobello", shouted Misha as she took off.

"MYEH-MYEH-MYEH-MYEH … MYEH-MYEH-MYEH-MYEH", echoed Gerard as he got back on his scooter.

When the Supercats arrived at the crossing on Portobello High Street, the girl who had pressed the button told them that the emergency was down on the promenade.

"My name is Zoe", she said, "My sister Kara needs your help".

They quickly sped down Bath Street and there outside the Espy Café on the corner they found Kara surrounded by a flurry of seagulls.

"They're trying to eat my chips!" she cried.

Sure enough, every few seconds a big seagull would swoop down and try to grab one of Kara's delicious chips.

Zoe had already eaten all of hers before the birds attacked.

"What can we do?" cried Zoe.

"MYEH-MYEH", said Gerard.

"What did he say?" asked Zoe.

Misha explained that Gerard suggested putting mustard on the chips. He'd seen it in a storybook. Seagulls don't like mustard.

"But I don't like mustard either", said Kara trying to stuff as many chips into her mouth as possible to stop the seagulls from getting them.

"We need to distract the seagulls", said Misha who then had a good idea.

Misha ran into the Espy Café and bought twelve long thin ice-lollies called ice-poles. There were six red strawberry ones and six green lime ones. She laid them out on the wall beside the beach and shouted to the seagulls:

"Look everyone!

SEAGULL LIGHT-SABRES!".

The seagulls all swooped down, picked up the lollies and started having a pretend battle between Seagull-Jedis and Seagull-Siths.

While the battle raged on, Kara gobbled up all her remaining chips in peace.

"Thanks very much, Misha Supercat ... and Gerard too, of course", she said.

On their way back home Misha pointed out to Gerard that they had made quite a lot of rescues which were not near pedestrian crossings. People had to meet them at the crossing and then take them to where they were needed.

"Not everyone lives near a main road. We must think of another way that people can alert us when they need help or advice", she said.

(What do you think they could do?)

(We'll find out next time!)

Chapter 8

Hi-Tec Alerts

As soon as they got home from Portobello, the two Supercats started to think about a new method that people could use to contact them.

They were sitting together in Misha's usual spot in the window of her flat. Mr Macdonald had just struggled up the stairs with a huge box in his arms.

"What's in there?" asked his wife.

"Oh, I bought a new microwave oven", he said, "The old one seems to be on the blink; it keeps pinging for no reason at all."

The two friends had a good laugh at silly Mr Macdonald.

Then they got down to serious business.

"Remember, not everyone lives near a pedestrian crossing. So it will need to be something that works everywhere", said Misha.

"Maybe we could have a 'Cat-Signal' like Batman's Bat-Signal", he suggested.

"How would people manage to project a cat symbol onto the sky?" she asked.

"Oh, yeah, I never thought of that", he said sheepishly.

Misha added, "And it will need to have the same features as the existing system.

Which are:

- If someone presses the button 3 times, it means that they have an emergency
- If they press the button 2 times, it means that they need advice

Gerard asked, "What does it mean if they press the button 1 time?"

"It means that they want to cross the road, of course!" she replied.

"Oh, yes, silly me (again)", said Gerard but then he had a good idea.

"What about a mobile phone app?" he said.

"That's brilliant!" said Misha.

Gerard was very pleased with himself and said that he would go down to his workshop straight away and start work on the new system.

Meanwhile, Mr Macdonald was cooking a bowl of porridge in the new microwave oven to test it out. There was a loud "PING" and he opened the door. A big cloud of steam came billowing out and he said:

"This one seems to be working fine. I'll chuck the old oven out for the bin-men tomorrow".

Misha just smiled and shook her head. "He's in for a shock the next time we're called out on an emergency mission and the mirror pings", she thought to herself.

After a few hours of hard work, Gerard called her down to his workshop to look at the new app.

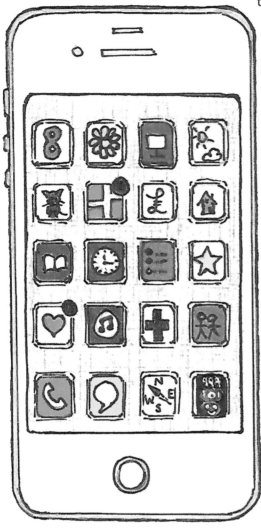

He showed Misha his phone. The app had three coloured circles on it: red, amber and green, just like a set of traffic lights.

The red circle had the number '999' written on it.

The amber circle had the number '101' on it and

The green circle had a 'smiley face' on it.

(Can you see the new app button in this picture?)

"That looks great", said Misha, "just like the police system. The red button is for emergencies, the amber button is for advice.

"But what's the third button with the smiley face for?"

(Can you guess what the third button is for?)

"Oh, the smiley face is for people to say 'Thanks for your help, Supercats'" he replied.

"Watch this ..."

Gerard pressed the green button and the picture of Auntie Kate winked and smiled.

Although they could not see it, a 'smiley face' appeared on the mirror upstairs too.

"If people are really pleased with us, they can press the green button lots of times, look!"

He pressed the button five times and with each press the smile on Auntie Kate's face got wider until she was grinning from cheek to cheek.

"Each press of the green button also makes a 'smiley face' appear on your mirror upstairs", he told Misha.

"Let's try the app now!" said Misha excitedly.

Gerard pressed the red button and they both heard the mirror upstairs go 'PING'.

Both shoes on the portrait of Auntie Kate flashed silver too.

He then pressed the amber button and they heard the mirror 'sneeze' and Auntie Kate's right shoe flashed.

"When someone presses these buttons, the app uses the phone's location to send a map to your mirror", Gerard explained.

"That all seems to be working well", said Misha.

Then Gerard got a bit carried away with himself.

He started pressing all the buttons ... a lot!

Red ... 'PING'

Amber ... 'ATISHOO'

Green ... 'Smiley Face'

Red ... 'PING'

Amber ... 'ATISHOO'

Green ... 'Smiley Face'

"STOP!" shouted Misha, "you'll be driving Mr and Mrs Macdonald crazy".

The Supercats decided that they would add details to their posters telling people how to download the new app for free.

When Misha went back upstairs to her flat, poor Mr Macdonald was busy packing up the new microwave oven into its original box and rescuing the old one from the bin.

"The new one seems to have the same trouble as the old one. No point in paying good money for the same old problem. I'll take this new one back to the shop tomorrow", he told his wife.

She did not hear him as she was busy opening a new pack of four boxes of paper tissues.

After hearing all the sneezes, she thought Mr Macdonald had a bad cold!

Chapter 9

Simple Solution

The new Supercats app was proving to be very popular with people who did not live near a crossing. The old method of calling for help was also available so that people without mobile phones could still contact the superheroes.

Mrs Macdonald was kept busy cleaning the mirror above the fireplace.

"I keep seeing big smudges in the mirror", she told her husband.

"They look a bit like 'smiley faces'".

"I clean the glass over and over but they keep coming back again".

"You could use some of the hundreds of tissues you've got lying around the flat", said Mr Macdonald.

"Is your cold not any better?" he asked.

"I don't have a cold. It's you that's got the cold; sneezing all day long", she replied. Mr Macdonald just shook his head and continued to do his crossword.

Misha Cat pretended to snooze and hoped that a map did not appear in the mirror while Mrs Macdonald was cleaning it. She would get a huge fright if it did!

Meanwhile, downstairs Gerard was still thinking about how to make his scooter go faster. The day before he had come up with what he thought was a 'great idea'. He tied a bit of string to Misha's leg and attached it to the front of his scooter. He asked Misha to fly off and he was dragged along behind her at great speed. But, as usual for Gerard, he had not thought it through properly!

He could not really steer the scooter when Misha was flying about.

He was dragged through several muddy puddles.

Gerard was covered in mud from head to toe.

"AARGH STOP", he cried but Misha could not hear him.

He tried to untie the string from his handlebars, but the knot was too tight.

He also forgot that Misha did not need to keep to paths and roads when she was flying.

Suddenly, Misha flew over the neighbour's garden and Gerard's scooter crashed into the fence.

The string snapped and Gerard ended up on his back in a flowerbed. Not such a 'great idea' after all.

"I'll never become a REAL Supercat!" he groaned.

Gerard pushed his scooter home and had a hot shower to wash the mud off of his fur.

His next 'great idea' was even crazier!

He thought about attaching two pigeons to the back of his scooter and feeding them beans.

The pigeons' pumpies would act like jet boosters and give him extra speed. There were many problems with this idea:

1. Beans need a while to take effect and Gerard needed to respond to emergencies very quickly.
2. He could not decide whether to use glue or string or Velcro to attach the pigeons to his scooter.
3. He could not find any pigeons willing to help him with his experiment.

Two pigeons were sitting on the window-sill looking into his workshop. They were very worried when they saw his plans on the drawing board. They looked at each other and gulped. They both coo-ed a big sigh of relief when they saw Gerard tear up his drawing and chuck it in the bin.

Gerard decided to take a break from inventing and remembered that he needed to wash his scooter.

It had got very muddy when he was dragged along before he crashed it into the fence.

He got a basin of hot, soapy water and washed off all the mud.

As he was drying his scooter, he saw an oil-can on the shelf in his workshop.

He squirted a little oil on the wheels of his scooter and noticed that they then spun round a lot easier than before.

Gerard decided to try it out. He found that his scooter went a lot faster than before and that he did not have to push quite so hard.

"Sometime the simplest solution is the best one", he thought.

Chapter 10

Goodness Beats Rudeness

One morning, the mirror pinged. There was an emergency!

Fortunately, Mr Macdonald was singing to himself in the shower so he did not hear it.

The mirror showed a map of the carpark at a big supermarket in Morningside.

The two Supercats sprang into action, meeting in the lane at the back of the garden.

"Destination Morningside", shouted Misha as she took off.

"MYEH-MYEH-MYEH-MYEH … MYEH-MYEH-MYEH", echoed Gerard as he jumped on his newly-oiled scooter and sped along keeping up with Misha.

When they got to the supermarket they found a very angry young man.

"My car is locked and the keys are inside", he shouted.

"How did that happen?" asked Misha.

"I put all my shopping into the boot of the car and then I shut it. I then found that the keys were inside beside the shopping bags", he complained.

"So, why do you think this is an emergency?" Misha asked him.

"I've just bought a large tub of ice-cream and it's going to melt if I don't get it home soon", said the man, "I hope it does not make a mess of my nice clean car boot. Oh, why did this have to happen to me?"

Misha had met this kind of person before; someone who was never to blame. Everything was always someone else's fault, no matter what happened.

"Tell me; who put the keys in the boot?" she asked.

"I did", he replied.

"And who closed the boot with the keys inside?"

"Well, I suppose I did", he said, still not admitting that he was to blame.

(*Very annoying!*)

He added "I can see the key through the back window, though". As if that helped to fix the problem!

Gerard got a hammer out of his rucksack and suggested to Misha that they should smash the back window to get to the key. The man did not understand what he said but, seeing the big hammer, he could guess what Gerard was planning to do.

"NOOOOOO!" shouted the man, "My precious car! You can't smash a window".

Gerard put the hammer back in his rucksack with a disappointed sigh. He would have LOVED to smash the window!

"Well, the only other way is to get another key. Do you have a spare one?" asked Misha.

"No, I don't. Do you think I would have called you out if I had a spare key?" he said, very rudely.

"OK then", she said, "We need to go to a garage and buy a new key. But, before we do that, we'll need to read the serial number off the key inside the car so that the garage will know which one we need".

"I can see the key, but the writing is too small to read from here", said the man.

Gerard took a magnifying glass from his tool-bag and was about to climb onto the roof of the car. His plan was to read the serial number on the key with the magnifying glass.

"NOOOOOO, you might scratch my paintwork with your claws. I can't have cats walking over my lovely car", said the man, huffily.

So, Misha used her cape to fly up over the car.

She held onto Gerard's legs while he dangled over the back window of the car with his magnifying glass in his hands.

"Hold steady", he said, "I can just about read it now".

"Be careful! Don't drop anything on my gorgeous car", said the very annoying man.

Finally, Gerard could read the serial number of the key and read it out to Misha, letter by letter.

"P-0-0-P-1-E P-4-N-T-5"

Misha and Gerard giggled at each other when they heard that it spelled out 'Poopie Pants'. She read it out to the man but he did not seem to think it was funny; he was too busy fretting over his car.

"What flavour of ice-cream is it?" Misha asked the man.

"Mint Choc Chip, if you must know!" he replied rudely.

Misha was starting to get fed up with this man as she flew off to the garage to get a new key for the car, leaving him and Gerard together.

"I hope she hurries up. I'm going to be late", thought the angry man.

"MMMMM, Mint Choc Chip, that's my favourite" thought Gerard to himself. He licked his lips as he leaned back against the car, thinking about its yummy minty-chocolatey taste.

"Don't touch my paintwork!" shouted the ungrateful man and Gerard moved away a bit. The man then produced a hanky and wiped the place where Gerard Cat had been leaning. Not a very nice thing to do!

Soon, Misha returned with the new key and they opened the boot of the car. The ice-cream was starting to get quite soft and ooze out of its tub. A few other frozen things were starting to thaw too.

"I suppose you may as well take these as they will be ruined by the time I get home", said the man as he reluctantly handed the ice-cream and some fish fingers to Misha and Gerard.

The Supercats decided to eat the ice-cream there and then before it melted any more. Gerard produced two spoons from his tool-bag and they scoffed it up while sitting on a bench.

While they were enjoying the treat, they heard the man complaining about being late for his work as if he were not to blame. He slammed the door of his car without thanking the Supercats who had helped him and sped off.

"What a rude man", said Gerard.

Just before he reached the exit of the carpark, his car skidded and crashed into a wall. The man got out of the car and screamed "My lovely car! Look at all the dents in my paintwork!"

When they got back home, Misha sneaked the pack of fish-fingers into the kitchen and left them beside the cooker.

Mrs Macdonald saw them and thought, "Mr Macdonald must have got these for Misha's lunch".

Mr Macdonald also saw the box and thought "Mrs Macdonald must have got these for Misha's lunch" and he cooked them all.

Gerard and Misha were very full indeed after eating all the fish-fingers and ice-cream.

Chapter 11

Gerard Sheep-Cat

Misha and Gerard were full of fish-fingers and ice-cream and were looking forward to a long snooze.

Misha had just got settled on her cushion and Gerard had just put his feet up on a stool in his workshop when the mirror made a loud 'PING'.

A map of Gorgie appeared.

Mr Macdonald was still in the kitchen, washing the lunch dishes. He gave the microwave oven a big thump on its top and shouted:

"GGGRRRRR! Stop that pinging, will you?"

Two seconds later, the mirror sneezed and both Mr and Mrs Macdonald said "Bless you my dear" at the same time!

When the mirror sneezed, the same map of Gorgie appeared again.

(Very strange: Two requests from the same place at the same time, one urgent and one not!)

The two Supercats dragged themselves out of their comfortable resting spots and headed, reluctantly, for the back garden.

When they met at the path, Gerard asked Misha if it was an emergency or not since there were two messages on the mirror.

"I'm not sure", she said, "but we'd better go to Gorgie and see what's happening".

They were both too full of yummy fish-fingers and ice-cream to fly or scoot along so they decided to take the bus.

They saw a number 1 bus coming and, as they got on it, Gerard said:

"MYEH-MYEH-MYEH-MYEH … MYEH-MYEH", to the driver.

"Eh, what was that?" said the driver.

"He said, 'Destination Gorgie'", explained Misha, "We'll get off at Gorgie Farm, please".

The bus driver kindly let them on the bus without paying since they were in their Supercat costumes.

"Thank you very much", said Misha

As they got near to Gorgie, the traffic was terrible; there was a huge queue of buses and cars blocking the road.

"What's going on here?" wondered Gerard out loud.

"Maybe it is an emergency after all!" shouted Misha, "Come on Gerard!"

The Supercats got off of the bus and ran past all the queueing vehicles to see what the problem was. When they got to Gorgie Farm, they soon found out.

There were about fifty sheep milling about on the road. They had escaped from their pen in the farm and were causing havoc with the traffic.

Some were eating the flowers from a lady's garden, one was chomping on some carrots from outside a shop and one was chewing a big lettuce which it had found in a rubbish bin.

The people who work at the farm were trying to get the sheep to go back up the lane where they had come from but it was no good. Every time one sheep looked as if it might go back, another would shoot off in a different direction.

"That's why we sent two messages to the Supercats", explained one of the farm workers, "we were not sure if it was urgent or not. We thought we could get the sheep back ourselves but the traffic kept building up and up. Please help up Misha Supercat", she pleaded.

Misha remembered seeing a programme about sheep-dogs on the TV and asked Gerard if he had a whistle in his tool-bag.

Gerard said, "Of course, I have everything in here". He found the whistle and gave it to her. Misha then gave some instructions to Gerard.

"You'll need to be the sheep-dog, or sheep-cat in your case, and I'll watch things from above", she said.

She climbed up on top of a bus shelter to look at the sea of sheep below.

There were sheep everywhere!

What a mess!

Misha and Gerard shouted **"Supercats to the rescue"** and they started their clean-up mission. Misha flew overhead, whistling directions to Gerard whenever she saw a naughty sheep. Gerard followed her instructions; darting here and there chasing all the woolly animals into small groups.

Eventually all the sheep gave up the battle for freedom and trotted back up the path to the farm, followed by Gerard Sheep-Cat. The road was now clear but there was quite a lot of rubbish left behind.

The farm workers said that they would tidy up the mess left by the naughty sheep.

"Well done Supercats!" everyone cheered and the traffic began to move again.

The lady who runs the café at the farm invited them both in to say 'thank you' for their help with the sheep.

"All that exercise has made me quite hungry again", said Gerard, "It's been nearly an hour since we had those fish-fingers".

As a reward, the café lady gave them both a bowl of soup and a cheese scone.

Chapter 12

Gerard Undercover

Gerard wanted to be more like Misha Supercat. He had enjoyed his success as a sheep-cat and he wanted to be the hero again. His dream was to become a real Supercat himself.

One day, he was in Pilrig Park, pretending that he was out on a solo mission. He would sneak around trying to surprise the squirrels and birds. They were the 'baddies' and he was the 'goodie'.

Gerard would hide behind a tree for a while and then shoot over the grass to another tree. He thought that if he ran really fast, the baddies would not see him until it was too late. Then he'd pounce on them and that would be that; they would be caught!

Of course, the birds and squirrels always saw him coming and managed to escape. When he pounced, there was nothing under his paws except grass or maybe a daisy or a buttercup.

Then, Gerard saw two boys sitting on a bench, talking.

"Let's get some sweets from the newsagent", said the bigger one, Rory.

"But, we've no money", said the other boy who was called Robbie.

"That's OK, we can just steal them when the man is not looking".

Gerard's ears pricked up when he heard this and Robbie noticed him standing nearby.

"Are you listening to us?" he asked.

"He's just a cat", said Rory, "they can't understand what we say. Can you, puss?"

Of course, Gerard <u>did</u> understand them and wanted to tell them it was wrong to take things without paying for them. When he tried to speak, all they heard was … "MYEH".

Since they didn't think that cats could understand them, they continued to make their plans while Gerard could hear them.

"How should we go about it?" asked Robbie.

"I've seen it on the TV", said Rory.

"<u>You'll</u> ask the man something about one of the magazines in the shop and then pretend to be interested in what he tells you. "

"While he's busy with you, <u>I'll</u> put some sweets in my pocket".

Gerard was shocked that these two were going to steal some sweets and so he decided he needed help from Misha Supercat.

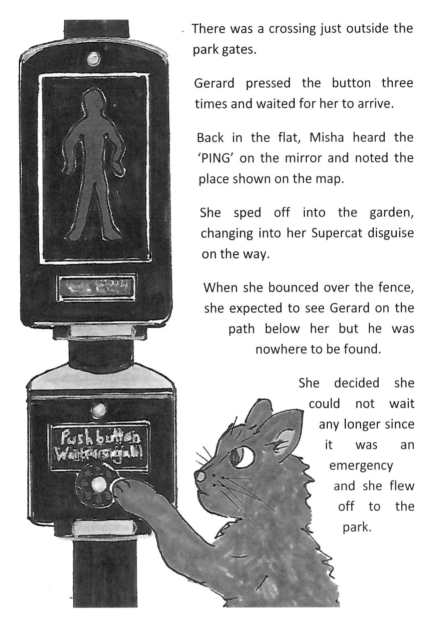

There was a crossing just outside the park gates.

Gerard pressed the button three times and waited for her to arrive.

Back in the flat, Misha heard the 'PING' on the mirror and noted the place shown on the map.

She sped off into the garden, changing into her Supercat disguise on the way.

When she bounced over the fence, she expected to see Gerard on the path below her but he was nowhere to be found.

She decided she could not wait any longer since it was an emergency and she flew off to the park.

"Destination Pilrig", she shouted and was sad not to hear Gerard's reply.

(What would Gerard have said?)

(That's right: "MYEH-MYEH-MYEH-MYEH … MYEH-MYEH")

"Where can Gerard be?" she thought as she flew along and then was very surprised to find him waiting for her at the crossing.

Gerard quickly explained to Misha what the two boys were planning.

"We can't arrest them until they actually steal something. There's always a chance that they will decide not to do it", she told Gerard. "Here's what we'll do …"

… and they made a plan!

Since Gerard did not have his disguise with him, they decided that he should use whatever was nearby to make him look different so that the two boys did not recognise him as the cat from the park.

He broke off a tree branch to make a walking stick and practised limping as if he had a sore leg. He found some white sand from the park's play pit and put it on his hair to make him look older, like his Grampa.

"I wish I had my tool-bag with me because I have a pair of glasses in it. Then they would never recognise me", he said.

"I'm sure you'll be fine", said Misha. "Quick! Here they come! Remember to give me the secret 'thumbs-up' sign if you see them stealing anything", she told Gerard and she hid herself around the corner.

When the two boys reached the door of the newsagent's shop, Gerard was pretending to have trouble opening it. Robbie held it open for him and said "There you go, you old cat".

They did not recognise him from the park; he was an undercover cat!

Gerard made a weak "MYEH" of thanks and limped inside.

Just as they had plotted, the Robbie showed the man a magazine which he had taken from the shelf and asked, "Excuse me Sir, is this the latest Ninjago magazine or is it the one from last month?"

As expected, the man went over to look and Rory took his chance. He stuffed his pockets full of freddos and fudges, mints and marshmallows.

Robbie put the magazine back on the shelf and said, "OK, thanks" to the man and then the two thieves headed for the door.

As they were leaving, Gerard tripped them up with his walking stick and they both fell on their faces on the pavement. The stolen sweets spilled out all over the place.

When they looked up, there was Misha Supercat with her 'MS' cape flapping behind her. Beside her they saw the old cat giving her the 'thumbs-up' sign.

(Can you make the 'thumbs-up' sign?)

Misha knew that this was their secret sign that the bad boys had stolen the sweeties.

"Are you going to pay for those sweets?" she asked, sternly.

"We haven't got any money", said Robbie.

"Well, put them all back immediately!" she shouted.

The boys said they were sorry and put the sweets back in the shop.

The shopkeeper was delighted and thanked Misha and the mysterious old cat who was with her.

He did not know that it was Gerard in disguise.

"But, how did you know that we were going take them?" Rory asked.

"That's an Undercover Supercat Secret", she said and winked at Gerard.

Chapter 13

Portrait Gallery

"Bless you, my dear", said Mrs Macdonald, "Is your cold no better today?"

The mirror had sneezed to tell Misha that there was a non-urgent request for the Supercats.

Downstairs, Gerard heard the sneeze and saw Auntie Kate's right shoe flashing. He finished his breakfast and wandered slowly out into the back garden.

He was putting on his mask and cape when Misha Supercat came down the drain-pipe. She did not bounce off the pond cover as it was not an emergency.

"What's the destination?" asked Gerard.

"The mirror showed a map of the Portrait Gallery in York Place", replied Misha, "Why don't you leave your scooter here and we'll take the bus again? We can get the 12 or the 26".

"I hope the 26 comes first", said Gerard, "I like to go upstairs and the 12s are usually single-decker buses".

Sadly, it was a 12 which came along and this made Gerard a bit grumpy.

"MYEH-MYEH-MYEH-MYEH … MYEH … MYEH", he said to the driver as he got on the bus.

"Eh? What did you say?" said the driver and this made Gerard even more grumpy.

"Destination York Place", said Misha. Gerard was beginning to get fed up with people not understanding him.

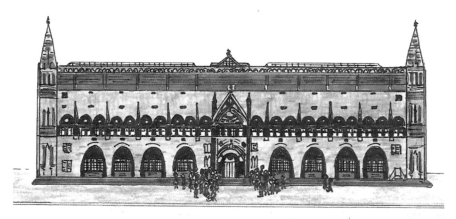

When they arrived at the Portrait Gallery, they were surprised to see a big crowd outside. They all started clapping and cheering as the two Supercats reached the door.

Inside the gallery, they saw the Mayor of Edinburgh. He was standing beside a large painting which had a sheet over the front of it.

"I'm pleased to unveil the latest portrait donated by the people of Edinburgh to thank two special friends for helping us out so much", he said grandly as he removed the sheet.

Behind the sheet was a huge painting of the Supercats in their costumes.

There, in the gallery, Misha was smiling broadly but Gerard was still annoyed about the bus being a 12 and the driver not understanding him.

Strangely, the two cats in the portrait had the same expressions; the portrait of Misha smiled while the portrait of Gerard looked grumpy.

When the mayor finished his speech, it was Misha's turn to talk.

She stood in front of the new portrait and started to thank everyone.

She got a bit carried away and Gerard thought she was really going to thank EVERYONE IN THE WORLD.

The expression on Gerard's face changed every time she mentioned someone:

(Can you make all these faces?)

Misha said, "I'd like to thank …"

- Gerard … for his wonderful inventions and assistance
  - He smiled (a little bit because he was still grumpy)
- Mrs Macdonald … for keeping the mirror clean
  - Gerard shook his head in surprise
- Mr Macdonald … for cooking our lunch
  - Gerard licked his lips and thought about fish-fingers
- The bus driver … for bringing us here today
  - Gerard looked confused and thought "Why thank <u>him</u>?"

Gerard noticed that when he made all these different faces, his portrait made the same faces too.

He then knew exactly what he needed to do to stop Misha from speaking!

He made the ugly face which his Grampa had taught him:

- He used his thumbs to pull his mouth wide open
- He pulled the bottom of his eyes down with his next fingers
- He pulled his nostrils up with his other fingers

  and finally

- He stuck out his tongue!

What an ugly face he made; and the portrait of Gerard made it too.

Everyone burst out laughing … except Misha.

She could not see the portrait because she was standing in front of it.

She did not understand what they were all laughing at.

When Misha looked over at Gerard, he quickly removed his hands and made an innocent face as if he had done nothing wrong. But, Misha knew him too well. She knew he had been up to something and she planned to pay him back!

After the speech, everyone went into the gallery café for tea and scones.

When the lady behind the counter asked Gerard if he wanted milk in his tea, he tried to say 'No' because he hates milky tea. The lady heard "MYEH" and did not understand.

Misha said "He said 'YES PLEASE' he loves milky tea." So the lady poured a lot of milk into Gerard's cup of tea.

Then she asked if Gerard wanted jam on his scone. This time, Gerard wanted to say "Yes" because he loves jam. When the lady heard "MYEH" again, she looked at Misha for help.

"He said he wants the jam spread all over his face because that's where it usually ends up anyway", said Misha with a cheeky smile.

"OK then", said the lady and spread the jam all over Gerard's face with a spoon!

"AAARRGHHH (MMMYYEHHH)", shouted Gerard and ran to the toilet to wash his face.

He could hear Misha laughing as he went out of the door.

Ah he passed the portrait on his way to the toilet, Gerard noticed that there was jam on his face up there too. It really was a strange portrait.

Misha came out of the café to say that she was sorry for playing a trick on him.

As she passed the new portrait, a huge dollop of jam fell off of the picture of Gerard's face and landed on her head.

"That serves you right", said Gerard and Misha had to agree.

They both laughed and decided to stop playing tricks on each other …

… for the moment anyway.

Chapter 14

The Translating Device

Gerard was still fed-up with people not understanding what he said. He was especially annoyed when Misha tricked him by telling people that he had said 'Yes' when he had really said 'No'.

He decided to learn to speak other languages.

"It's alright for Misha", he complained to himself, "That's one of her Supercat superpowers. I don't have any superpowers".

He borrowed a book called a dictionary from Mr Macdonald. The book had lots of words with pictures beside them. You could look at what was in the picture and learn how to say its name by reading the letters in the word. The books started with things beginning with the letter 'A', like APPLE, ANT, AEROPLANE, APRICOT and ALLIGATOR.

"What a lot of words!" he exclaimed, "and I haven't even got to the letter 'B' yet. It will take me ages to get to CAT or DOG, never mind ZEBRA".

He was beginning to wish he had never started this project.

"I'm no good at learning languages", he said, "The only thing I'm good at is making things with my tools".

That gave him another 'great idea'!

"I'll invent a machine which translates 'cat language' into words which other people can understand. Then I won't need Misha to tell them what I'm saying", he thought, excitedly.

At first, Gerard thought about making another phone app which would translate his cat-words like "MYEH" and MYEH-MYEH" into words people could understand. He soon realised that people would see him holding his phone and he really wanted people to think he could actually speak their language. So, he made the device look like a badge on his mask!

(Can you see it in the picture?)

Gerard spent the whole afternoon building a device which would fit into the mask of his Supercat costume. It would listen to what Gerard said in cat language and translate it into human language.

First, the device would have to learn all the words in the dictionary book which Gerard had borrowed from Mr Macdonald.

He set the device up to take photographs of all of the pages in the dictionary and store the information in its memory.

Gerard had to turn a page over after each photograph was taken.

As you know, he is a bit clumsy and sometimes he turned over two or three pages at a time. This meant that some words were missing from his translating device. So, when he tried to say those words, only silence would come out.

His lips would be moving but there would be no sound.

(Can you do that?)

By mistake, he also managed to stick some pages together with jam from the sandwich which he was eating for his lunch. This meant that some words were stuck together in the device:

- If he tried to say 'carpet' the device would say 'carpet-cartoon'
- It he tried to say 'cup' the device would say 'cup-cupboard'
- If he tried to say 'picnic' the device would say 'picnic-pie-poopoo-pumpie-pants'.
    - There was a LOT of jam on those pages!

Gerard was also having sausages for his lunch and he often dropped one onto the book just as a photograph was being taken.

This meant that the word 'sausage' appeared more often than normal in his human language.

When it was ready, Gerard decided to try it out in his workshop. He pretended to meet Mrs Macdonald at the shops. He said:

"Good morning, Mrs Macdonald. That's a lovely hat you're wearing today" in cat language into his mask. The device said:

"Good morning, Mrs Macdonald. That's a lovely sausage you're wearing today"!

"Oh well", he sighed, "Nothing's perfect. It's only the first version of my Translation Device. I'll call it 'TD1'".

He decided to try out TD1 the next time the Supercats were called out on a mission.

It would be a big surprise for Misha ...

... Gerard could speak to other people!

Chapter 15

Gerard Speaks to Humans!

The next day, the Supercats were called out on a non-urgent mission.

Gerard was very excited when he met Misha at the back gate. He had his mask on and the translating device (TD1) was installed and ready to go.

It still had a few problems but Gerard could not wait to try it out.

He had not switched on the device yet so when Misha took off and shouted, "Destination Balerno", Gerard still said "MYEH-MYEH-MYEH-MYEH … MYEH-MYEH-MYEH" …

… but Misha could understand him.

It was just humans who could not … or so Misha thought!

When they arrived at Balerno, they found a lady waiting for them.

She wanted to know the best way to build a tent in her back garden for her children to play in.

Gerard switched on the device when no-one was looking.

Misha was just about to answer, when Gerard whispered, "MYEH … MYEH" into TD1.

The device then said (quite loudly):

"I think a good way to make a tent is to put a big sheet over the backs of four chairs and hold it in place with some clothes-pegs".

Misha was astonished!

She stared at Gerard with her mouth wide open. When she finally managed to speak, she said "WOW! When did you learn to speak to people, Gerard?"

"Oh, it's just something I can do now", he said in cat-language. He did not tell Misha about the device in his mask.

The lady thought that was a good way to make a tent and said, "What should we put on the floor of the tent?"

Gerard spoke and the device said:

"You could use an old bit of carpet-cartoon".

The lady was a bit confused.

"Should they have anything to drink in the tent?" she asked.

"Oh yes" said Gerard, **"They could have a cup-cupboard of milk".**

The lady was even more confused and was getting a little bit annoyed with Gerard. She thought he was just being silly.

"What about something to eat?" she asked, "What would you suggest to eat in a tent?"

(You know what Gerard is going to say now?)

He wanted to say, "They could have a picnic", but the device said:

"They could have a picnic-pie-poopoo-pumpie-pants".

Then he tried to say, "They could sit on some pillows" but this was one of the pages he had dropped a sausage onto so he actually said:

"They could sit on some SAUSAGES".

Next Gerard suggested that the children could play a game of cards, but sadly 'cards' was on one of the pages he missed out so the device said:

"They could play a game of _____".

"What?" said the lady, getting a bit angry.

She could see his lips moving but could not hear anything.

"They could play a game of _____", replied Gerard.

"A game of WHAT?" shouted the lady again.

"A game of _____", replied Gerard.

The lady was furious and walked away saying:

"That's the last time I'll ask the Supercats for advice!"

Misha was very surprised by what she had heard him say so she asked Gerard what was going on.

He told her about the translating device and said he would try to fix the problems with it.

"The next version 'TD2' will be much better", he promised Misha.

"OK, for the moment, just try not to say 'picnic' to Mrs Macdonald, please", said Misha.

"Why not?" asked Gerard.

"Because you would say 'picnic-pie-poopoo-pumpie-pants' instead and Mrs Macdonald would find that very, very rude", replied Misha.

"OK, I'll make sure I fix the word 'picnic' first in 'TD2'. I borrowed a dictionary from Mr Macdonald", said Gerard.

"Well you should make sure you give him it back because he needs it to complete his crossword", said Misha.

"Oh, that reminds me", said Gerard, "I've made up a crossword in human language for Mr Macdonald. I know how he likes to do them every day".

Gerard produced a bit of paper with this on it:

			S	A	U	S	A	G	E	S			
										A		E	
										U		G	
E	G	G	S			S				S		G	
			A		S	A	U	S	A	G	E	S	
			U			U				G			
S	A	U	S	A	G	E	S			E			
A			A			A				S			S
U			G		E	G	G	S			E		A
S			E			E					G		U
A			S			S	A	U	S	A	G	E	S
G			E								S		A
E			G										G
S	A	U	S	A	G	E	S						E
			S							E	G	G	S

Most of the answers were 'sausages' but 6 words were not.

(Can you find them?)

Chapter 16

Double Trouble

Mr Macdonald had spent all morning waiting beside the microwave hoping to catch it out. "I'll find out what's going on with this crazy machine even if I have to stand in the kitchen all day", he told his wife.

She just shook her head and got on with her knitting.

Then, something very unusual happened. There were two calls for the Supercats at the same time. One was urgent and the other was not. This had only happened once before; when the sheep were running about on the road.

(Do you remember that mission?)

The Gorgie Farm workers did not know if it was urgent or not so they sent in two different requests for the same location.

This time the missions were in two different places!

The mirror pinged and then sneezed very quickly. As soon as he heard the 'PING', Mr Macdonald opened the door of the oven and looked inside. When the mirror then sneezed, Mrs Macdonald shouted at him.

"Stop sneezing in the microwave", she cried, "I don't want all your germs on my food".

"But, I didn't", he replied.

"Yes, you did. I heard you", said his wife and she shooed him out of the kitchen. She started to wipe the oven with a clean cloth, muttering to herself. Mr Macdonald sat in his chair and muttered to himself too.

"What a day", he said, "and the crossword is a bit strange today too".

Fortunately, Misha Cat had been watching the mirror when this all happened and she saw the two different maps appear. The emergency was at Ainslie Park Swimming Pool and someone wanted help and advice in Holyrood Park.

When the Supercats met at the back of the garden, Misha said that she would fly off to Ainslie Park and Gerard should go to Holyrood Park on his scooter.

Gerard decided to do his destination announcement in human language for the first time but he soon discovered that he had dropped one of his lunch sausages on the page with the word 'park' on it. Instead of shouting "Destination Holyrood Park", he shouted …

(Can you guess what he shouted?)

That's right; he shouted **"Destination Holyrood Sausage"** and set off at speed on his scooter.

Misha thought this was very funny, so she bounced on the trampoline and shouted "Destination Ainslie Sausage" as she flew off to the rescue.

When she arrived at Ainslie Sausage … I mean Ainslie Park, she found a lady by the side of the pool.

She was very unhappy.

"My baby has dropped her sheetie in the pool and it has sunk right to the bottom", she sobbed.

"What's a sheetie?" asked Misha

"It's a muslin cloth that she needs to hold when she's going to sleep", the lady replied.

"Don't worry. I'll get it", said Misha Supercat. She took off her cape since she only needs it for flying and she did not want it to get wet. She practised holding her breath and counting to ten, to make sure she would have enough air to make the rescue.

At the same time, Gerard had arrived in Holyrood Hamburger … I mean Holyrood Sausage … I mean Holyrood Park.

There he met a man who had a flat tyre on his ice-cream van.

(Can you see which tyre is flat?)

He needed help to change the wheel.

Gerard found a jack in his toolbag-rucksack and used it to lift the van's flat tyre off of the ground.

While Gerard worked away at the wheel, the man continued to sell ice-creams to a long line of children who were waiting.

Everything was going so well:

- Misha was ready to rescue the sheetie
- Gerard was about the change the wheel

What could go wrong? …

… Find out next time.

Chapter 17

Double Rescue

Misha and Gerard were on separate missions. Gerard was changing a wheel on an ice-cream van in Holyrood Hotdog … Hamburger … Sausage … Park.

Misha Supercat was about to make a daring, underwater rescue at the swimming pool.

She took a big breath and dived into the water. She swam down to the bottom of the pool to try to find the sheetie. It was very difficult because the sheetie was white and so was the bottom of the pool.

She managed to catch it with her clooks just as she was running out of air and swam back up to the surface.

Misha took a big gulp of air as soon as her face was out of the water.

The lady was very pleased but then she noticed that the sheetie was soaking wet.

"Please help me to dry it as my baby needs to have an afternoon nap soon", she pleaded.

Misha said she knew of a great place to dry the sheetie: the flagpole on the top of Edinburgh Castle.

She put on her cape and told the lady to go into the changing room to get herself and her baby dressed.

"It's very windy at the top of the castle. The sheetie will be dry in no time. I'll be back by the time you are ready to leave", she said as she flew off across the city to tie the sheetie to the flagpole.

When she got up to the top of the castle, she could see all the way over the city to where Gerard was working.

"I wonder how he's getting on. I hope he has managed OK on his own. Accidents seem to happen to Gerard … a lot", she thought to herself.

Gerard had just replaced the wheel and was unwinding the jack to let the van back down. As soon as the new round wheel was on the ground, the van started to roll forward.

It was running down the hill! There was no-one in the driving seat as the man was still in the back selling ice-cream!

The van rolled faster and faster down the slope. Gerard ran after it but he could not catch it. Ice-creams and chocolate bars were flying out of the window and the children were picking them up.

It was their lucky day; they were delighted to get free goodies!

The man in the van was not so pleased. "HELP", he shouted, "Somebody help me!" as the van headed for the pond at the bottom of the hill. Big white swans were scattering in all directions, covered in raspberry sauce and chocolate sprinkles.

Misha Supercat saw all of this from the top of the castle and zoomed to the rescue. Just as the van was about to splash into the pond, she caught it and made it stop.

"Oh, thank you!" said the man gratefully as he pressed the green smiley-face button on his phone app ten times. He then started tidying up the mess inside the van.

The swans were washing themselves in the pond to get all the sticky mess off of their feathers.

Gerard arrived and said, "Sorry, I should have checked that the brake was on before changing the wheel. No wonder I'm not a real Supercat."

"Never mind", said Misha, "No harm done. Keep trying and someday you might make it. Then you would get a real cape."

"Oh, that would be my dream come true", said Gerard.

"I'll see you back at home, Gerard", said Misha as she took off.

Misha had to fly back to Edinburgh Castle to collect the sheetie, which was nice and dry.

She arrived at the pool just as the lady was coming out of the building with her sleepy baby.

By the time she got back home Misha was very tired.

"You've been out for a long time, Misha", said Mrs Macdonald as she gave her a bowl of lovely warm milk.

"Look at that mirror! There are ten smudges on the glass and I cleaned it only this morning".

"All in a day's work", thought Misha as she lapped up her milk.

Chapter 18

Lazy Sunday Afternoon

It was a quiet Sunday afternoon in the Macdonald household.

Misha Cat was having her usual snooze in the window of the flat. She was having real difficulty in keeping awake because the poached salmon she had had for her lunch was making her very sleepy.

"I suppose the mirror will wake me up if there is a mission", she thought as she slowly fell asleep.

Mrs Macdonald was pottering about in the garden, cutting the grass and picking weeds out of the flower-beds.

Her husband was in the flat, tidying up after lunch. He had washed and dried the dishes, always keeping one eye on the microwave oven in case it 'tried any of its tricks'.

Next he got out the vacuum cleaner to pick up all the crumbs off the carpet. As he was doing this, his favourite song came on the radio and he started to sing and dance about.

It was the song from the Lego Movie.

(Do you know that song? It's called 'Everything is Awesome')

As he stepped back, his bottom accidentally pressed the secret button behind the curtains. This is the one which Misha uses to get out of the flat for emergency missions. Mr Macdonald was too busy dancing and singing to notice the window opening by itself.

Down in the garden, the drain-pipe started to swing out over the grass towards the pond. Mrs Macdonald had just bent over to pick a weed out of the grass when the drain-pipe hit her on the bottom.

She fell over face-first and landed in the pond with a splash!

The trampoline cover started to slide out over the pond so she had to scramble out quickly before it covered her up.

By the time Mrs Macdonald got out of the pond, covered in mud, the drain-pipe had gone back against the wall so she had no idea what had pushed her into the water.

She climbed back up the stairs to the flat to change out of her wet clothes and have a shower.

"Everything is awesome!" sang Mr Macdonald.

"GGRRRRRR I'll give you 'awesome'!" said Mrs Macdonald.

"Everything is cool when you're part of a team!" sang Mr Macdonald not realising that his wife was not pleased.

"GGRRRRRR I'll give you 'part of a team'!" said Mrs Macdonald and slammed the bathroom door.

Meanwhile, Gerard was downstairs in his workshop updating the translating device he had made to help him speak other languages. He was trying to find all the 'sausage' words to replace them with the correct ones. This would be version 'TD2'.

He was drinking a glass of milk as he did this.

As you know, Gerard is very clumsy and he knocked the glass with his elbow by mistake. Some milk spilled on the floor and Gerard bent down to wipe up the mess. He bent over just as the device was changing the word 'football' in human language and it took a picture of his bottom!

Gerard was too busy to notice this so he did not know that any time he wanted to say 'football' to a human he would say **'bottom'** instead!

(I can't wait to hear what happens, can you?)

The mirror sneezed and Mrs Macdonald shouted from the bathroom:

"Typical! I'm the one who falls into the pond and gets soaking wet and he's the one who gets a cold".

Mr Macdonald just ignored her. "She's crazy", he thought to himself.

Misha woke up and looked at the mirror. It showed a map of Inverleith Park.

When they took off on the mission, Misha shouted "Destination Inverleith Park" and Gerard shouted .....

(Can you guess?)

He shouted **"Destination Inverleith Park"** too since he had fixed the 'sausage' problem for the word 'park'.

When they arrived at the park they saw lots of men playing football.

One team was playing in light blue strips and the other was in red. The 'blues' were called 'Inverleith City' and the 'reds' were called 'Inverleith United'. The captain of the 'blues' came over and said that he had called the Supercats using the app on his phone.

"Hi, my name is Thomas Slim", he said, "I'm the captain of Inverleith City Football Club".

"We have a problem here".

"A big dog ran onto the pitch and stole the ball".

"It picked up the football in its mouth and ran away", he explained.

"This is an important match and we need to finish it but we don't have a spare ball".

Gerard looked into his marvellous tool-bag and found a football. He took it out and gave it to the man saying:

"Here you are. I'm happy for you to kick my bottom for the rest of the match!"

"What!" said Thomas; shocked.

"My bottom", said Gerard, **"it's big and round and you and your friends can kick it really hard. I don't mind".**

Thomas thanked the Supercats and walked away shaking his head.

The referee blew his whistle and the game started again.

Gerard then spoke to Misha in cat-language, saying: "They can keep that football as I have another one at home. It's handy to have more than one football in case you lose one".

Misha said, "I'm glad you did not tell <u>him</u> that in human language. He would have heard you saying that you have another bottom at home and that you like having more than one bottom in case you lose one".

Then she added, "I think your translation device still needs a bit more work, Gerard. You should maybe make version 'TD3'".

Chapter 19

Christmas Lights

It was nearly Christmas-time and the nights were very dark in Edinburgh. People had put up trees and lights in their houses.

Mrs Macdonald had put fairy lights all around the mirror above the fireplace. She was humming along to the 'Snowman' music on the radio.

She had deliberately worn her oldest cardigan with holes in the sleeves hoping that Mr Macdonald would take the hint and buy her a new one for Christmas. She was not too hopeful since she had not seen any parcels that looked like a cardigan under the tree.

Mr Macdonald sat in his chair in front of the fire pretending he was doing his crossword as usual. He was wearing a Christmas pudding jumper and his favourite pair of tartan slippers. They were very old and had a few holes in them but they were very comfortable. He loved his old slippers.

He hoped that Mrs Macdonald had not bought him a new pair for his Christmas but he had seen a suspiciously 'slipper-shaped' parcel with his name on it under the tree.

Eventually, Mr Macdonald dozed off and had a snooze.

Gerard was downstairs in his workshop trying to untangle the lights for his tree. The wires looked like a spider's web. "I wish I'd put them away properly last year", he grumbled to himself.

Mrs Macdonald was in the kitchen making shortbread in the shape of holly leaves and stars. She likes to give these to her friends as presents along with some of her home-made raspberry liqueur.

Misha was in her usual spot by the window thinking that she might ask Santa for a new cushion.

Suddenly there was a loud 'PING' and a map of the Botanical Gardens appeared in the mirror. Downstairs, Gerard's Auntie Kate's shoes were both flashing silver.

There was an emergency!

Mr Macdonald woke up with a start and ran into the kitchen. He opened the door of the microwave and found it empty, again.

"That's strange", he said, "and I can smell cooking too".

"That's because I'm using the other oven", said his wife, "Go back to sleep".

"I wasn't sleeping", he insisted, "just resting my eyes".

Misha Supercat and Gerard met at the back gate. Gerard had fitted a big bright torch to the front of this scooter so that he could see in the dark.

"Destination Botanics", said Misha Supercat as she took off into the inky blue sky. Her cape lit up when she was flying at night so that people could see her coming.

"MYEH-MYEH-MYEH-MYEH … MYEH-MYEH-MYEH!" shouted Gerard. He had given up trying to speak human language when there was just Misha there. She always laughed when he got things wrong so he decided to speak 'cat'.

When they arrived at the gardens, there was a huge commotion going on. Lots of people were queuing at the gate, waiting to get in but the gates were closed.

Along came a man with a badge which said:

"Harris L. Baxter

Head of Garden Entertainment"

Harris explained to Misha that there was supposed to be a big Christmas lights show there. Hundreds of people had bought tickets to come along and wander around amongst the plants and trees which were covered with different coloured lights.

"There's supposed to be Christmas music playing too", Harris said.

"So, what's wrong?" asked Misha.

"Something has gone wrong with the electricity. It's all gone off", he explained.

Harris added that he was worried that people who were already inside the gardens could not see anything.

Just then, they heard a loud splash and a yell as a man stepped off the path and fell into a pond.

"We'll see what we can do to help", said Misha, "I'll make sure everyone in the garden is safe. Gerard, you use your tools to see if you can fix the electricity problem".

Misha flew off over the gardens, guiding people to safety.

Lots of clever children had brought torches with them. Some had them on their heads and others had multi-coloured torches on their fingers. One girl even had a glowing light-sabre and was using it as a torch while her mother helped her father to climb out of the pond.

Gerard went quickly into the big building beside the gate to see if he could work out what the problem was. He went past the shop and the rooms where you can learn about plants.

Everything looked different when lit only by the light of his torch. He was more used to being there on sunny summer days when he liked to chase squirrels around the gardens.

He went into the café where he could smell some delicious toast.

A man was sitting drinking a cup of tea and spreading peanut butter on the toast.

Beside the toaster was a big plug with large writing on it:

"BOTANIC LIGHTS - DO NOT UNPLUG"

It was unplugged!

The man had taken out the plug so that he could plug in the toaster to make his supper.

Gerard quickly disconnected the toaster from the socket.

"But I might want some more toast", wailed the man.

"Well, you can plug the toaster in somewhere else if you want more toast", said Gerard through his latest translating device, 'TD176'.

(He had been making a LOT of changes to his device, hadn't he?)

He reconnected the 'lights' plug and immediately he heard music blaring from loud-speakers somewhere outside.

Gerard warned the man not to unplug the lights again, even if it was a toast emergency.

When he went back out into the garden, Gerard saw a magical wonderland of flickering lights and sparkling baubles.

The light show was back on!

Everyone clapped and cheered as Gerard came out of the building.

Misha was very proud of him.

"You are getting very close to earning your Supercat cape", she said.

Gerard was very excited! He REALLY wanted to be a Supercat, just like Misha.

The two friends spent a wonderful evening enjoying the magnificent display of lights and synchronised music.

The Botanics Lights event was a great success, all thanks to Gerard.

(Have a look at the spectacular glass-house on the next page!)

(See how many different colours you can find in the picture.)

Chapter 20

Superhero Supermarket

It was Christmas Eve and everyone was getting ready for Santa's arrival. All of the children who had been 'good' had sent their letters to Santa. Some of them who had been 'not so good' had also sent letters … just in case.

Mrs Macdonald was in a bad mood because there was still no 'cardigan-shaped' parcel under the tree. There would be no humming of Christmas songs today!

Misha was hoping that there would be no missions today or tomorrow. She wanted a quiet Christmas holiday. She was looking forward to having some yummy turkey for her Christmas dinner.

Mrs Macdonald had invited Gerard for the meal too; she just did not know it yet. Misha had told Gerard to come up to visit on Christmas Day and they both knew that kind Mrs Macdonald would give him some food.

But Misha did not get her wish for a peaceful rest …

Suddenly, the mirror pinged and Auntie Kate's shoes flashed. The Supercats were needed somewhere! The map on the mirror showed a big square in the centre of Edinburgh, St Andrew Square.

When the friends met at the back gate they were surprised to find that it was very windy.

"Be careful flying in this storm", said Gerard to Misha.

"I will", replied Misha, "See you in St Andrew Square".

Gerard had no idea if she shouted her usual 'Destination' thing because the wind was howling in his ears and he could not hear anything.

When he arrived at the site of the emergency, Misha was already there.

She was talking to a man who had a hard-hat on his head.

He showed Misha a large building surrounded by scaffolding.

The workmen use this scaffolding to climb to the top of the building when they are working on it. The man explained what the emergency was:

"One of the builders has left a wheel-barrow full of bricks up on the scaffold. The men are all off on holiday now and I'm worried that this wind will blow it over. It could hurt someone if it falls on them."

"Leave it to me", said Misha as she flew off. She was just about to land on the top of the building when a strong gust of wind blew her off balance.

She banged into one of the scaffolding poles and fell onto the wooden platform at the top of the building.

The pole had ripped her Supercat cape and she could not fly anymore!

She had also hurt her leg and could not walk.

Gerard saw all of this and immediately sprang into action. He left his scooter at the bottom of the scaffold and started to climb up.

It was very dangerous because the wind was making the scaffold shake about a lot.

Brave Gerard finally reached the top where Misha lay on her side, her torn cape flapping about in the strong wind.

"Are you OK, Misha?" asked Gerard.

"I've hurt my leg and ripped my cape. I don't know how I'll get down", she replied.

"Don't worry; I'm here to help", said Gerard, bravely.

The wind was still howling and the scaffolding was shaking dangerously.

(I hope they are going to be OK, don't you?)

Slowly, Gerard managed to help Misha down to the ground. She still could not fly and her leg was very sore.

"I'll take you home on my scooter", said Gerard.

"No, I'll need to buy a new cape right away in case there are other emergencies", replied Misha, "I'll show you where we get them".

Misha got onto Gerard's Scooter behind him and they went to a big shop.

The sign outside the shop said:

"SUPERHERO SUPERMARKET"

Gerard was amazed. "I've never seen this shop before", he exclaimed.

"It's only for real superheroes", said Misha as she got off of the scooter.

Gerard was a bit annoyed that Misha pointed out that he was not a real superhero and that <u>his</u> cape was just an old curtain.

"I'll see you at home then", he said and he turned to leave. He was shocked to find that his scooter was all bent.

It was not meant to have two cats on it and their weight had damaged it quite badly.

Gerard had to walk all the way home, feeling quite sad.

However, the next day was Christmas Day!

As arranged, Gerard came upstairs to visit Misha who was looking very pleased with herself for some reason.

"Oh, hello, Gerard", said Mrs Macdonald, "It's nice to see you. Merry Christmas. Would you like to have some turkey?"

"MYEH", said Gerard, too scared to try speaking human-language in case he said something rude.

(Anyway, remember that the Macdonalds think that Misha and Gerard are both just ordinary cats so they would have had a huge shock if Gerard had spoken to them.)

After lunch, Mrs and Mrs Macdonald opened their presents.

Mrs Macdonald was surprised when she got a lovely new pink cardigan.

"I hid it inside a shoe-box so that you would not know what it was. I know that you like to 'squeeze' parcels under the tree", said her husband with a smile.

Mr Macdonald opened his parcel and, sadly, it was a new pair of slippers.

"Don't worry", said his wife, "I've kept the receipt and you can change them for a crossword book if you want".

The two cats went downstairs to Gerard's workshop and Misha showed Gerard the new cape she had bought for herself at the Superhero Supermarket. Gerard said it was very nice but he still felt a bit jealous of Misha.

She gave Gerard a parcel and said, "This is to say 'thank you' for saving me last night. I'm sorry that your scooter was damaged. Perhaps this will make up for it."

Gerard opened the parcel and was amazed at what he saw. Inside was a REAL golden superhero cape with the letters 'GS' sewn onto it.

"Merry Christmas, GERARD SUPERCAT; a REAL SUPERHERO", said Misha.

More Bedtime Stories

The Rabbit with Three Ears

The Rabbit with Three Ears gets up to tricks with other rabbits, pigeons, a seagull, a fox, a dog, a mole and a cat.

Martha, the Magical Mouse

Martha the Mouse discovers that she can do magical things (sometimes).

She and her musical friend, Mary, have lots of adventures in London and elsewhere.

She visits her cousin Trevor, the Rabbit with Three Ears, during the Edinburgh Festival and they all take a camping trip to the island of Arran.

43516054R00056

Printed in Poland
by Amazon Fulfillment
Poland Sp. z o.o., Wrocław